THE ANIMAL PARADE

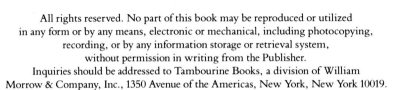

Library of Congress Cataloging in Publication Data

King-Smith, Dick. The animal parade/by Dick King-Smith; illustrated by Jocelyn Wild. —1st U.S. ed.   p.   cm.
Summary: A collection of animal stories, fables, and poems.   1. Animals—Literary collections.
[1. Animals—Literary collections.]   I. Wild, Jocelyn, ill.   II. Title.
PZ5.K57556An   1992   91-30332   CIP   AC   ISBN 0-688-11375-3

Printed and bound in Hong Kong
1 3 5 7 9 10 8 6 4 2
First U.S. edition

THE ANIMAL PARADE

A COLLECTION OF STORIES AND POEMS

Selected and written by
Dick King-Smith

illustrated by
Jocelyn Wild

TAMBOURINE BOOKS · NEW YORK

Contents

To the reader

Of all the animal stories that I've read, there are a number that have stuck in my mind. I enjoyed them at first reading, and the enjoyment of each book, or each story, or just a particular bit of a story has stayed with me, and grown.

From that number I've chosen a few pieces that between them give me—and I hope will give you—everything a story should. Some are comical, some very funny, some are dramatic, exciting, frightening even, some sad, some indeed tragic.

These selections are quite simply my particular favorites.

Also, just for fun, I've chosen five of Aesop's Fables and put them in my own words.

To all these, because I'm a writer of animal stories, I've added some bits from my own books, and I've written some verses that might make you smile. I'd sooner see you laugh than cry.

Dick King-Smith

The Country Mouse and the City Mouse

by Aesop

More than two and a half thousand years ago, a Greek slave called Aesop wrote a collection of fables. These were stories mainly about a whole lot of different animals and their treatment of one another. Every story carries a moral—a lesson. And now, just as in those far-distant days, everyone can learn something from those lessons.

Two Mice who had been playfellows as youngsters decided, when they grew up, on different ways of life.

One went to live in a great house in a large city. The other retired to the country to live in a hole in a garden bank.

One fine evening, the Country Mouse was sitting at the entrance to his hole, enjoying the smell of the flowers and the song of the birds and the sight of the fields and the woods and the mountains, when who should appear on a visit but his old friend, the City Mouse.

"Come in! Come in!" cried the Country Mouse. "How good to see you! You must be hungry and tired from your journey. Sit down! Sit down! Supper will be served in just a moment."

And in just a moment the Country Mouse set before the visitor some moldy gray peas, some bacon rinds, a little coarse oatmeal, some cheese-parings, and the core of a ripe apple.

To ensure that the City Mouse had all he needed, the

Country Mouse, saying that he had dined earlier, ate nothing but sat and nibbled on a wheatstraw.

When the City Mouse had had enough (which was soon, for the simple fare was not to his taste), he said, politely but nonetheless firmly, "Now don't take offense, old fellow, but tell me–how can you bear to live in this damp dark hole eating moldy gray peas, with nothing to smell but all those flowers, nothing to hear but all those songbirds, and nothing to see but fields and woods and mountains? Why not come and stay with me in town? You'll find you'll much prefer it."

The Country Mouse did not particularly care for the idea, but good manners made him agree, and they set out together. Once inside the great house, the City Mouse made his friend comfortable in the middle of a magnificent Persian carpet, and set before him a great many courses of delicious, expensive, and beautifully-prepared tidbits and sweetmeats.

The Country Mouse was enjoying this feast, and

beginning to think that he had been missing out on life's luxuries, when suddenly someone opened the dining-room door, and the two Mice heard the sound of deep barking, a sound that grew louder and louder until into the room galloped a great Mastiff.

"Oh my word!" cried the Country Mouse to the City Mouse as they fled from the dog. "If this is town life, you can keep it! Me, I'm off back to my damp dark hole and my moldy gray peas!"

MORAL: *Be satisfied with what you've got; trying for better things may leave you worse off in the end.*

The Wind in the Willows

by Kenneth Grahame

*The Water Rat and the Mole have been for a long walk.
Suddenly the Mole knows for certain that he is close to his old home,
which he had forsaken and to which he had never returned since first he
found the river. He longs to search for it, to go to it, but Ratty, by now far
ahead, calls him on, and on the Mole loyally goes. But he can
no longer control his misery at having to leave "Mole End" behind.*

Poor Mole at last gave up the struggle, and cried freely and helplessly and openly, now that he knew it was all over and he had lost what he could hardly be said to have found.

The Rat, astonished and dismayed at the violence of Mole's paroxysm of grief, did not dare to speak for a while. At last he said, very quietly and sympathetically, "What is it, old fellow? Whatever can be the matter? Tell us your trouble, and let me see what I can do."

Poor Mole found it difficult to get any words out between the upheavals of his chest that followed one upon another so quickly and held back speech and choked it as it came. "I know it's a–shabby, dingy little place," he sobbed forth at last, brokenly: "not like–your cozy quarters–or Toad's beautiful hall–or Badger's great house–but it was my own little home–and I was fond of it–and I went away and forgot all about it–and then I smelt it suddenly–on the road, when I called and you wouldn't listen, Rat–and everything came back to me with a rush–and I *wanted* it!–O dear, O dear!–and when you *wouldn't* turn back, Ratty–and I had to

16

leave it, though I was smelling it all the time—I thought my heart would break. We might have just gone and had one look at it, Ratty—only one look—it was close by—but you wouldn't turn back, Ratty, you wouldn't turn back! O dear, O dear!"

Recollection brought fresh waves of sorrow, and sobs again took full charge of him, preventing further speech.

The Rat stared straight in front of him, saying nothing, only patting Mole gently on the shoulder. After a time he muttered gloomily, "I see it all now! What a *pig* I have been!

A pig—that's me! Just a pig—a plain pig!"

He waited till Mole's sobs became gradually less stormy and more rhythmical; he waited till at last sniffs were frequent and sobs only intermittent. Then he rose from his seat, and, remarking carelessly, "Well, now we'd really better be getting on, old chap!" set off up the road again, over the toilsome way they had come.

"Wherever are you (hic) going to (hic), Ratty?" cried the tearful Mole, looking up in alarm.

"We're going to find that home of yours, old fellow," replied the Rat pleasantly; "so you had better come along, for it will take some finding, and we shall want your nose."

Never give your guinea pig
Marmalade or jam,
Never give it Mars Bars,
Never give it Spam.
Fetch it no fish-fingers,
Bring it no baked beans;
Only give your guinea pig
Greens, greens, greens.

Dick King-Smith

The Sow and the Wolf

by Aesop

A Sow had recently farrowed, and lay in the straw of her sty, happily nursing her newborn piglets. Suddenly she heard a noise.

She looked up to see a Wolf resting its forefeet on top of the pig-sty wall and peering over.

"What a lovely picture!" said the Wolf in a smarmy voice. "A mother and her children! A handsomer mother or more beautiful children I have never seen. And so many! You have ten, madam, I declare!"

The Sow grunted. The Wolf, she noticed, had a tendency to dribble as he spoke.

"How pink and plump they are!" the Wolf went on. "How delicious they look! But what a strain it must be upon you, to have to cope with so many. You will need a break, I feel sure–a chance to get away from the duties of motherhood."

The Sow grunted again.

"Allow me to make a suggestion," said the Wolf. "Why not let me baby-sit for you? Then you could go for a walk and stretch your legs, confident that your little ones would be attended to in your absence."

At this the Sow got to her feet, very carefully so as not to harm any of her piglets, and walked ponderously forward to look up at the Wolf leaning upon the pig-sty wall.

"How good of you to offer to attend to my children," she

said politely. "And now be good enough to listen carefully to what I have to say. Take your nasty hairy feet off my wall, and keep your nasty long nose out of my affairs or I'll bite it off."

MORAL: *If strangers offer you anything—say "No."*

Johnny Bear

by Ernest Thompson Seton

*Some of my choices are from animal books that were written a very
long time ago, when my father was a small boy.
The story of Johnny Bear, for example, was first published in
1901, and it looks as though children were expected to understand
very long words in those days. So you may have to persevere.
What does that mean, did you say? Look it up in the dictionary.*

Thus, they came close to the kitchen, and there, in the last
tree, Johnny's courage as a leader gave out, so he remained
aloft and expressed his hankering for tarts in a woebegone
wail.

It is not likely that Grumpy knew exactly what her son
was crying for. But it is sure that as soon as she showed an
inclination to go back into the pines, Johnny protested in
such an outrageous and heartrending screeching that his
mother simply could not leave him, and he showed no sign
of coming down to be led away.

Grumpy herself was fond of plum jam. The odor was
now, of course, very strong and proportionately alluring; so
Grumpy followed it somewhat cautiously up to the kitchen
door.

There was nothing surprising about this. The rule of "live
and let live" is so strictly enforced in the Park that the Bears
often come to the kitchen door for pickings, and on getting
something, they go quietly back to the woods. Doubtless
Johnny and Grumpy would each have got their tart but that a
new factor appeared in the case.

That week the Hotel people had brought a new Cat from
the East. She was not much more than a kitten, but still had a
litter of her own, and at the moment that Grumpy reached
the door, the Cat and her family were sunning themselves on
the top step. Pussy opened her eyes to see this huge, shaggy
monster towering above her.

The Cat had never before seen a Bear–she had not been there long enough; she did not know even what a Bear was. She knew what a Dog was, and here was a bigger, more awful bobtailed black dog than ever she had dreamed of coming right at her. Her first thought was to fly for her life. But her next was for the kittens. She must take care of them. She must at least cover their retreat. So, like a brave little mother, she braced herself on that doorstep, and spreading her back, her claws, her tail, and everything she had to spread, she screamed out at that Bear an unmistakable order to

STOP!

The language must have been "Cat," but the meaning was clear to the Bear; for those who saw it maintain stoutly that Grumpy not only stopped, but she also conformed to the custom of the country and in token of surrender held up her hands.

However, the position she thus took made her so high that the Cat seemed tiny in the distance below. Old Grumpy had faced a Grizzly once, and was she now to be held up by a miserable little spike-tailed skunk no bigger than a mouthful? She was ashamed of herself, especially when a wail from Johnny smote on her ear and reminded her of her plain duty, as well as supplied his usual moral support.

So she dropped down on her front feet to proceed.

Again the Cat shrieked, "STOP!"

But Grumpy ignored the command. A scared mew from a kitten nerved the Cat, and she launched her ultimatum, which ultimatum was herself. Eighteen sharp claws, a mouthful of keen teeth, had Pussy, and she worked them all with a desperate will when she landed on Grumpy's bare, bald, sensitive nose, just the spot of all where the Bear could not stand it, and then worked backward to a point outside the sweep of Grumpy's claws. After one or two vain attempts to shake the spotted fury off, old Grumpy did just as most creatures would have done under the circumstances: She turned tail and bolted out of the enemy's country into her own woods.

But Puss's fighting blood was up. She was not content with repelling the enemy; she wanted to inflict a crushing defeat, to achieve an absolute and final rout. And however fast old Grumpy might go, it did not count, for the Cat was still on top, working her teeth and claws like a little demon. Grumpy, always erratic, now became panic-stricken. The trail of the pair was flecked with tufts of long black hair, and

there was even bloodshed (in the fiftieth degree). Honor surely was satisfied, but Pussy was not. Round and round they had gone in the mad race. Grumpy was frantic, absolutely humiliated, and ready to make any terms; but Pussy seemed deaf to her cough-like yelps, and no one knows how far the Cat might have ridden that day had not Johnny unwittingly put a new idea into his mother's head by bawling in his best style from the top of his last tree, which tree Grumpy made for and scrambled up.

This was so clearly the enemy's country and in view of his reinforcements that the Cat wisely decided to follow no farther. She jumped from the climbing Bear to the ground, and then mounted sentry-guard below, marching around with tail in the air, daring that Bear to come down. Then the kittens came out and sat around, and enjoyed it all hugely. And the mountaineers assured me that the Bears would have been kept up the tree till they were starved, had not the cook of the Hotel come out and called off his Cat—although this statement was not among those vouched for by the officers of the Park.

Alice's Adventures in Wonderland

by Lewis Carroll

Alice comes upon a March Hare and a Mad Hatter having tea at a table under a tree. They are resting their elbows on a sleeping Dormouse and talking over its head. At last they pinch it to wake it.

The Dormouse slowly opened his eyes. "I wasn't asleep," he said in a hoarse, feeble voice; "I heard every word you fellows were saying."

"Tell us a story!" said the March Hare.

"Yes, please do!" pleaded Alice.

"And be quick about it," added the Hatter, "or you'll be asleep again before it's done."

"Once upon a time there were three little sisters," the Dormouse began in a great hurry, "and their names were Elsie, Lacie, and Tillie; and they lived at the bottom of a well—"

"What did they live on?" said Alice, who always took a great interest in questions of eating and drinking.

"They lived on treacle," said the Dormouse, after thinking a minute or two.

"They couldn't have done that, you know," Alice gently remarked, "they'd have been ill."

"So they were," said the Dormouse, "*very* ill."

Alice tried to fancy to herself what such an extraordinary way of living would be like, but it puzzled her too much, so she went on: "But why did they live at the bottom of a well?"

"Take some more tea," the March Hare said to Alice, very earnestly.

"I've had nothing yet," Alice replied in an offended tone, "so I can't take more."

"You mean you can't take *less*," said the Hatter, "It's very easy to take *more* than nothing."

"Nobody asked *your* opinion," said Alice.

"Who's making personal remarks now?" the Hatter asked triumphantly.

Alice did not quite know what to say to this, so she helped herself to some tea and bread-and–butter, and then turned to the Dormouse, and repeated her question. "Why did they live at the bottom of a well?"

The Dormouse again took a minute or two to think about it, and then said, "It was a treacle well."

"There's no such thing!" Alice was beginning very angrily, but the Hatter and the March Hare went "Sh! Sh!" and the Dormouse sulkily remarked, "If you can't be civil, you'd better finish the story for yourself."

"No, please go on!" Alice said. "I won't interrupt again. I dare say there may be *one*."

"One, indeed!" said the Dormouse indignantly. However, he consented to go on. "And so these three little sisters–they were learning to draw, you know—"

"What did they draw?" said Alice, quite forgetting her promise.

"Treacle," said the Dormouse, without considering at all this time.

"I want a clean cup," interrupted the Hatter, "let's all move one place on."

He moved on as he spoke, and the Dormouse followed him. The March Hare moved into the Dormouse's place, and Alice rather unwillingly took the place of the March Hare. The Hatter was the only one who got any advantage from the change, and Alice was a good deal worse off, as the March Hare had just upset the milk jug into his plate.

Alice did not wish to offend the Dormouse again, so she began very cautiously, "But I don't understand. Where did they draw the treacle from?"

"You can draw water out of a water well," said the Hatter, "so I should think you could draw treacle out of a treacle well–eh, stupid?"

Three Cautionary Verses

by Dick King-Smith

*I've written some verses which, I suppose, carry a moral
(though I don't know what Aesop would think of them!)
I'm all for your having sensible sorts of pets, but just in case you
should be tempted to try keeping an out-of-the-way kind of animal,
read on and* BEWARE.

A girl who lived in Birkenhead
And kept a tiger in a shed
Lived (for a short while) to regret
That she had chosen such a pet.
It wasn't that the stripy beast
Was fierce (not in the very least—
Quite tame in fact). The trouble lay
In what a lot it ate each day.
She had a job, try as she might,
To satisfy its appetite,
For fifty cans of Kit-E-Kat
Each morning weren't enough for that.
At last she learned the thing they do
With all the tigers at the Zoo:
Six days a week they give them meat,
But not one bite of food to eat
On Sundays. "Good idea, my friend!"
She said, and at the next weekend
She left the cat food on the shelf;
But then the tiger helped itself
(Not to the cans, it must be said,
But to the girl from Birkenhead).

A lion with lots of curly hair
And penetrating teeth
Was given to a prankish pair
Of twins, who lived in Neath.

No sooner was the lion indoors
Than, for a joke, the two
Thrust both their heads between its jaws
As lion tamers do.

The difference between such men
And this misguided twain
Is that the lion tamers then
Remove their heads again.

A girl who lived in Wensleydale
Acquired an alligator (male—
Or so she thought until it laid
A dozen eggs). The girl, dismayed,
Suspected that her parents might
Be less than happy at the sight
Of thirteen alligators' heads
Agape among the flower beds.
When Mom and Dad were fast asleep,
She crept out to the compost heap,
With trowel and fork began to delve,
And buried the offending twelve.
Alas, the little girl was not
Aware that compost heaps are hot,
And in this warm and cozy state
The eggs began to incubate
Until there were, one sunny morn,
Twelve little alligators born
Which ran into the countryside,
And grew, and grew, and multiplied.
So, if in Wensleydale, beware
And always take a lot of care.
You could be out to buy some cheese
And lose your legs below the knees.

The Hodgeheg

by Dick King-Smith

Max, the Hodgeheg, is a young hedgehog determined to find a safe way for his kind to cross roads. He has an unfortunate experience on a crosswalk, which accounts for the spelling of the title of this story. A huge truck has just driven clean over him without touching him.

The sheer horror of this great monster passing above with its huge wheels on either side of him threw Max into a blind panic, and he made for the end of the crossing as fast as his legs would carry him. He did not see the cyclist silently pedaling along close to the curb and the cyclist did not see him until the last moment. Feverishly the man twisted his handlebars, and the front wheel of the bicycle suddenly wrenched round, caught Max on the rump, and catapulted him head first into the face of the curbstone.

The next thing that Max recalled was crawling painfully under his own front gate. Somehow he had managed to come back over the crosswalk. He had known nothing of the concern of the cyclist, who had dismounted, peered at what looked like a small dead hedgehog, sighed, and pedaled sadly away. He remembered nothing of his journey home, wobbling dazedly along on the now deserted pavement, guided only by his sense of smell. All he knew was that he had an awful headache.

The family had crowded round him on his return, all talking at once.

"Where have you been all this time?" asked Ma.

"Are you all right, son?" asked Pa.

"Did you cross the road?" they both said, and Peony, Pansy, and Petunia echoed, "Did you? Did you? Did you?"

For a while Max did not reply. His thoughts were muddled, and when he did speak, his words were muddled too.

"I got a head on the bump," he said slowly.

The family looked at one another.

"Something bot me on the hittom," said Max, "and then I headed my bang. My ache bads headly."

"But did you cross the road?" cried his sisters.

"Yes," said Max wearily. "I hound where the fumans cross over, but—"

"But do you mean the traffic only stops if you're a human?" interrupted Pa.

"Yes," said Max. "*Not* if you're a hodgeheg."

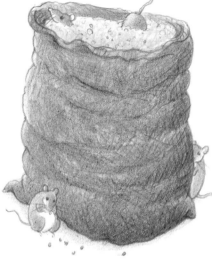

Five Eyes

In Hans's old Mill his three black cats
Watch his bins for the thieving rats.
Whisker and claw, they crouch in the night,
Their five eyes smoldering green and bright:
Squeaks from the flour sacks, squeaks from where
The cold wind stirs on the empty stair,
Squeaking and scampering, everywhere.
Then down they pounce, now in, now out,
At whisking tail, and sniffing snout;
While lean old Hans he snores away
Till peep of light at break of day;
Then up he climbs to his creaking mill,
Out come his cats all gray with meal—
Jekkel, and Jessup, and one-eyed Jill.

Walter de la Mare

Tarka the Otter

by Henry Williamson

Young otters, like young children, have to learn to swim, but they do so very quickly. And what fun it is! The baby Tarka rejoices in this new and exciting element.

When he went into the water the next night and tried to walk toward his mother, he floated. He was so pleased that he set out across the river by himself, finding that he could turn easily toward his mother by swinging his hindquarters and rudder. He turned and turned many times in his happiness, east toward Willow Island and the water song, west toward the kingfisher's nest, and Peal Rock below Canal Bridge, and the otter path crossing the big bend. North again and then southwest, where the gales came from, up and down, backward and forward, sometimes swallowing water, at other times sniffing it up his nose, sneezing, spitting, coughing, but always swimming. He learned to hold his nose above the ream, or ripple, pushed in front of it.

While swimming in this happy way, he noticed the moon. It danced on the water just before his nose. Often he had seen the moon, just outside the hollow tree, and had tried to touch it with a paw. Now he tried to bite it, but it swam away from him. He chased it. It wriggled like a silver fish and he followed to the sedges on the far bank of the river, but it no longer wriggled. It was waiting to play with him. Across the river Tarka could hear the mewing of his sisters, but he set off after the moon over the meadow. He ran among buttercups and cuckoo-flowers and grasses bending with bright points. Farther and farther from the river he ran, the moonlight gleaming on his coat.

As he stopped to listen to the bleat of lambs, a moth whirred by his head and tickled him. While he was scratching, a bird flying with irregular wingbeats and sudden hawklike glidings took the moth in its wide gape and flew out of his sight.

Harry's Mad

by Dick King-Smith

Harry's Mad (the African Grey parrot, Madison) has a wonderful gift of speech and understanding. Harry knows this secret. As yet, his parents do not.

"It's a pity they haven't got proper brains like us, isn't it, Dad? I mean, he could help you with the *Sunday Times* crossword puzzle."

"Don't be silly, Harry," said his mother, and to her husband, "off you go and settle down with your precious puzzle. Harry, time for you to do the washing up, please. Put Madison back in his cage first."

"Yes, Mom," Harry said.

In the passage between kitchen and sitting room he stopped for a moment, out of earshot of both parents.

"Mad," he said softly.

"Yeah, Harry?"

"Shall we let them in on the secret now?"

"I sure hope so, Harry boy. It's kinda weird, just repeating stuff all the time. Makes me feel like a real dope."

"OK, Mad," said Harry. "But wait till I've finished the washing up. I don't want to miss this."

He went on into the sitting room where his father was already settled, pipe in mouth, pencil poised, and put Madison into his cage.

"I hope that bird's going to keep quiet now," Mr. Holdsworth said.

"Oh he will, Dad," said Harry, grinning. "I'm sure."

"Sure," said Madison.

Time passed, and all was Sunday morning peace and silence. The only small sounds were the occasional scratch of Harry's father's pencil, the noise of a page turning as his mother read a book, and the cracking of seeds in the parrot cage. Harry came in with the mugs of coffee.

At that moment Mr. Holdsworth knocked out his pipe and sighed deeply.

Mrs. Holdsworth closed her book. "Are you stuck?" she said.

"Mm. It's quite a hard one today really. Listen to this for instance. I can't think of a single word in the English language that fits. Blank S two blanks T blank C blank N blank."

"What's the clue?"

"'Cat in spite of being a bird.'"

There was a moment's silence, and then, "It's an anagram, Mr. Holdsworth, sir," said Madison in a respectful voice. "'Psittacine.' Means, 'belonging to the parrot family.' You want I should spell it for you?"

The Fox and the Sick Lion

by Aesop

The Lion, King of Beasts, was ill, so ill, it was said, that he was unable to leave the cave which was his home.

"Have you heard the news?" the other animals said to one another. "His Majesty is sick!"

"Too weak to leave his cave, they say!"

"Yet he wishes us all to visit him!"

"What an honor!"

"How gracious!"

"He will look kindly, it is said, upon all who call."

And so each animal in turn made its way to the Lion's cave to pay their respects to their Sovereign.

Only the Fox did not go.

After a while the Lion summoned the Jackal.

"Listen, fleabag," he growled. "I've got a job for you."

"Yes, sire. Certainly, sire. Whatever you say, sire," whined the Jackal.

"Go and fetch the Fox," said the Lion. "Almost all my subjects have come to visit me in my hour of need, except the Fox. Has he no manners? Has he no courtesy? Has he no respect?"

"I don't know, I'm sure, sire," said the Jackal.

"Well, go and ask him, ratfink!" roared the Lion in a voice that sounded remarkably strong for an invalid.

So the Jackal hurried off to find the Fox and give him the royal message.

"You'd better get a move on," he said. "His Majesty's none too pleased."

The Fox cleaned his whiskers thoughtfully.

"I don't know about manners and courtesy and respect," he said, "but I do know how many beans make five. I've had a little look around the entrance to the royal abode, and I noticed a funny thing. There are many footprints of many different beasts in the sand outside the mouth of the cave, and they all have something in common."

"What's that?" asked the Jackal.

"They all point forward," said the Fox. "All those footprints point into the cave but none of those feet, it seems, ever came out again. If the Lion is indeed ill, it can only be from one cause."

"What's that?" asked the Jackal.

"Indigestion," said the Fox, and he trotted away in the opposite direction.

> *MORAL:* *You can learn by other people's mistakes.*

More Cautionary Verses

by Dick King-Smith

A little girl who came from Crewe,
And longed to own a horse,
Instead was treated to a gnu
(Or wildebeeste, of course).

The gnu appeared extremely old
And had a job to stand.
(The little girl had not been told
That it was secondhand.)

Within a week the gnu had died.
She wept to see it fall.
"I gnu it all the time!" she cried.
"It wasn't gnu at all!"

A noisy boy who came from Slough
Was always making such a row
It nearly drove the neighbor mad.
"Can't you control your little lad?"
He asked the youngster's Mom and Dad.

So they decided they would get
The boy a python as a pet.
They told the neighbor what they'd done—
"The snake will give him hours of fun!
No longer will you hear our son."

How right they were! The little lout
Not only let his python out—
He slipped it in next door. Around
The neighbor's neck the python wound:
He never heard another sound.

A little boy from Leigh-on-Sea
Was given, for a present,
A large and hairy chimpanzee
By nature so unpleasant,

That those who tried to pet the beast,
Or stroke it, like a kitten,
Were sure, to say the very least,
To be severely bitten,

And relatives who chanced to come
Were not disposed to linger—
A second cousin lost his thumb,
An aunt her little finger.

The boy was sad. His parents too.
"The ape must go," said Mother.
They sent the creature to the Zoo
And bought the boy another.

This chimp, by contrast, seemed a dear,
So quiet it was, so gentle;
It kissed his granny on the ear
(Which made her sentimental).

The little boy it carried round
As though he were a dolly,
And while the ape stayed on the ground
Why, that was very jolly!

Till one day, with the lad a-perch,
In front of all the people
Of Leigh-on-Sea, it climbed the church
And chucked him off the steeple.

Daggie Dogfoot

by Dick King-Smith

Daggie Dogfoot thinks he can fly. He finds that he can't, and falls into the brook. But pigs can't swim either, or so his Mammie told him! Then he hears the voice of his friend, Felicity the Muscovy duck. "Run after me," she says. "Just run as though you were on dry land."

Because of the confidence in the duck's voice, because he had spirit and courage still in the midst of his panic, and because there was nothing else to do, Daggie obeyed. He clenched his teeth together, tipped up his head so that his nostrils pointed skyward like the twin guns of a surfaced submarine, kicked with his hindlegs and paddled like mad with his doggy feet, trying hard to imagine that he was galloping through the grass.

To his amazement, he began to move forward through the water after the duck, at first slowly, then faster as he gained momentum and confidence, and finally so fast that before they reached the far bank he was level with her and they touched bottom together in a little reedy inlet.

They looked at one another and their eyes shone, Felicity's with amusement and pleasure, Daggie's with relief and triumph as realization swept over him.

"Pigs can't fly," said Daggie. Felicity shook her head.

"But there's one pig," said Daggie quietly, "that can—" said Daggie more loudly, "swim!" shouted Daggie Dogfoot at the top of his squeaky voice, and off he set, all by himself, toward his mother on the Resthaven bank.

Mrs. Barleylove had continued throughout to yell "Save my boy!" pausing only when it seemed he had reached safety. Now here he was back in deep water again, and she began to squeal as before, until two voices reached her ears.

"Calm yourself, missus," said one as the duck, who had flown quickly across over the head of the swimmer, landed beside her. "He's all right. Just listen to him." And as the sow quietened, she heard the other voice, the voice of her fast-approaching son.

"Mammie! Mammie!" came the cry over the gentle lapping of the pool. "Look at me! I can swim! It's easy!

Watch!" And as she stared, open-mouthed, the small figure came paddling nearer and nearer, pushing up a little bow wave in front of it with the speed of its progress.

Still Mrs. Barleylove did not really understand what had happened since the sun had woken her. As soon as Daggie was out of the brook and shaking himself like a water-spaniel, she turned and made off up the bank toward the summit, scolding as she went in the way that mothers do when their children have given them a bad fright.

"Silly boy!" she said. "Naughty boy! Come quickly and run about in the sunshine or you'll catch your death of cold. I told you not to go down by the water. You're never to go there again, d'you understand? Never. I don't know what your father would say if he knew," and so on, until, receiving no reply, she turned and found that she had been talking to herself.

Below her, as she stood at the take-off point on the top of the high bank, two figures swam happily about the pool. One was white with black patches, and one was white with black spots, and as Mrs. Barleylove watched giddily from the height, they made a series of patterns in the pool, first one leading, then the other. Circles they made, and figures-of-eight, and zigzags, and criss-crosses, till the surface frothed and little wavelets lapped and slapped against the banks.

Slowly the incredible truth dawned upon Mrs. Barleylove. Her poor undersized deformed child was swimming, really swimming, swimming beautifully. 'Special feet for some purpose', eh? If only the neighbors could see him now.

"Oh, Daggie my love!" she called down. "How clever you be!"

How happy I am, thought Daggie, to have such a lovely mother, to swim in this beautiful sparkling stuff, to be with my friend whose very name means happiness. And he paddled madly about, while every little fish in the pool formed its mouth into a perfect round o of wonder. The moorhens in the reeds tut-tutted their amazement. The heron on the top of a downstream willow squawked his disbelief. A brilliant kingfisher gave an admiring whistle, and a passing green woodpecker laughed hysterically. And up the line of the brook flew a solitary swan, the sound of his great wings expressing exactly the surprise of all. "Gosh!" was the noise they made. "Gosh! Gosh! Gosh! Gosh!"

Your baby brother looks like a gorilla?
There, there! Now, now! Tut, tut! You mustn't cry.
Remember ev'ry ugly caterpillar
Becomes a very handsome butterfly.

Dick King-Smith

The Frog of Droitwich Spa

by Dick King-Smith

A boy who lived in Droitwich Spa
Kept lots of tadpoles in a jar,
And every evening, for a treat,
He fed them little bits of meat.

Now though they simply loved the stuff,
For one of them t'was not enough,
And (I expect that you can guess)
Each night there was one tadpole less.

Till out of those the jar contained
Only the cannibal remained.
He grew some legs and lost his tail,
Moved from the jar into a pail,

And then into the bath, because
So large a frog by now he was.
So large and, what is more, so fierce,
With teeth, that though they did not pierce,

Could give a most unpleasant nip.
One evening, with a bulldog grip,
He grabbed his
owner's father's toe.
"That's it!" cried Dad.
"He'll have to go!"

The boy from Droitwich Spa thought hard—
He'd make a pretty useful guard—
That lightning leap, those clamping jaws
Would make the boldest burglar pause.

"I'll write a notice out," he said.
He nailed it on the gate. It read
GUARD–FROG PATROLLING DAY AND NIGHT!
BEWARE! FROG WILL ATTACK ON SIGHT!

The postman laughed until he cried.
No sooner had he stepped inside
Than with a sudden mighty jump
The guard-frog bit him in the rump.

The milkman suffered just the same,
And so indeed did all who came.
And as for burglars, why, they said
They'd try another house instead,

Seeing behind the garden gate—
His bulging eyes ablaze with hate—
The most ferocious frog by far
That ever dwelt in Droitwich Spa.

Elephant Bill

by J.H. Williams

You would have thought that nothing could trouble an animal as huge and powerful as an elephant. But the forces of Nature are far stronger than any mere beast.

But one of the most intelligent acts I ever witnessed an elephant perform did not concern its work, and might just as well have been the act of a wild animal.

One evening, when the Upper Taungdwin river was in heavy spate, I was listening and hoping to hear the boom and roar of timber coming from upstream. Directly below my camp the banks of the river were steep and rocky and twelve to fifteen feet high. About fifty yards away on the other side, the bank was made up of ledges of shale strata. Although it was already nearly dusk, by watching these ledges being successively submerged, I was trying to judge how fast the water was rising.

I was suddenly alarmed by hearing an elephant roaring as though frightened, and, looking down, I saw three or four men rushing up and down on the opposite bank in a state of great excitement. I realized at once that something was wrong, and ran down to the edge of the near bank and there saw Ma Shwe (Miss Gold) with her three-month-old calf, trapped in the fast-rising torrent. She herself was still in her depth, as the water was about six feet deep. But there was a life-and-death struggle going on. Her calf was screaming with terror and was afloat like a cork. Ma Shwe was as near to the far bank as she could get, holding her whole body against the raging and increasing torrent, and keeping the calf pressed against her massive body. Every now and then the swirling water would sweep the calf away; then, with terrific strength, she would encircle it with her trunk and pull it upstream to rest against her body again.

There was a sudden rise in the water, as if a two-foot bore had come down, and the calf was washed clean over the

mother's hindquarters and was gone. She turned to chase it, like an otter after a fish, but she had traveled about fifty yards downstream and, plunging and sometimes afloat, had crossed to my side of the river, before she had caught up with it and got it back. For what seemed minutes, she pinned the calf with her head and trunk against the rocky bank. Then, with a really gigantic effort, she picked it up in her trunk and reared up until she was half standing on her hind legs, so as to be able to place it on a narrow shelf of rock, five feet above the flood level.

Having accomplished this, she fell back into the raging torrent, and she herself went away like a cork. She well knew that she would now have a fight to save her own life, as, less than three hundred yards below where she had stowed her calf in safety, there was a gorge. If she were carried down, it would be certain death. I knew, as well as she did, that there was one spot between her and the gorge where she could get up the bank, but it was on the other side from where she had put her calf. By that time, my chief interest was in the calf. It stood, tucked up, shivering and terrified on a ledge just wide enough to hold its feet. Its little fat, protruding belly was tightly pressed against the bank.

While I was peering over at it from about eight feet above, wondering what I could do next, I heard the grandest sounds of a mother's love I can remember. Ma Shwe had crossed the river and got up the bank, and was making her way back as fast as she could, calling the whole time—a defiant roar, but to her calf it was music. The two little ears, like little maps of India, were cocked forward, listening to the only sound that mattered, the call of her mother.

Any wild schemes which had raced through my head of recovering the calf by ropes disappeared as fast as I had formed them, when I saw Ma Shwe emerge from the jungle and appear on the opposite bank. When she saw her calf, she stopped roaring and began rumbling, a never-to-be-forgotten sound, not unlike that made by a very high-powered car when accelerating. It is the sound of pleasure, like a cat's purring, and delighted she must have been to see her calf still in the same spot, where she had put her half an hour before.

As darkness fell, the muffled boom of floating logs hitting against each other came from upstream. A torrential rain was falling, and the river still separated the mother and her calf. I decided that I could do nothing but wait and see what happened. Twice before turning in for the night I went down to the bank and picked out the calf with my torch, but this seemed to disturb it, so I went away.

It was just as well I did, because at dawn Ma Shwe and her calf were together–both on the far bank. The spate had subsided to a mere foot of dirty-colored water. No one in the camp had seen Ma Shwe recover her calf, but she must have lifted it down from the ledge in the same way as she had put it there.

Five years later, when the calf came to be named, the Burmans christened it May Yay Yee (Miss Laughing Water).

Confusion

Some bullfrogs must be cowfrogs,
And—just like cock and hen—
Some cockatoos are henatoos,
Some ladybirds are men.

Dick King-Smith

Noah's Brother

by Dick King-Smith

Noah's brother was left behind when the gang plank of the Ark was raised, and would have been drowned by the rising waters had not his friends the white doves, Peace and Goodwill, spotted him. One of the two pythons then swam out and coiled itself around the old man and hoisted him aboard, one of the elephants sucked the water out of him with its trunk, and one of the gorillas thumped his chest to get his heart beating again. Then all the animals got together to see what they could do for Yessah.

So, at last, Yessah sat down to eat a splendid breakfast, deep in the lowest, darkest part of the belly of the Ark.

He drank thirstily from a great pitcher of warm buffalo milk, and chewed hungrily on the radishes. Then he swallowed the grapes whole, pips and all. Finally he ate a raw egg. Which may not sound like much, but it was an ostrich's egg.

"Lovely!" he said, rubbing his tummy. "Now I simply must sleep. I can't keep my eyes open."

"Not yet, Yessah," said the bull elephant, "first a bath." He stuck his trunk out of a porthole and sucked, then squirted a great jet of water over Yessah, again and again, till all the dirt and filth was washed away. Now Yessah stood clean but shivering in his soaking-wet clothes.

"We'll soon warm you up," said one of the grizzly bears, and took the little man in her arms, hugging him very carefully against her hot, hairy chest until he was as dry as a bone.

"Now you can sleep, Master," cooed Peace and Goodwill, and Yessah saw that the most comfortable bed you can
imagine had been made for him.

For a mattress, there were two great tigers, lying back to
back; Yessah stretched himself between them, upon the
striped velvet of their glowing hides. He rested his weary
head on a pillow of warm, furry wolfskin (with a wolf

inside it). Just as he was dropping off to sleep, he felt as though the lightest, softest coverlet had been pulled over him to keep him cozy, for down fluttered a blanket of little birds—finches, robins, wrens, and many more, one pair of each—and they settled gently upon Noah's brother, spreading their small wings over him.

Beetle in Your Boots

Is there a beetle in your boots?
You'd better look and see.
Although you may not give two hoots,
The beetle will give three.

Dick King-Smith

The Jungle Book

by Rudyard Kipling

This is the final meeting between Mowgli, the jungle boy brought up by the wolves, and Shere Khan the lame tiger, his great enemy. Shere Khan has eaten and drunk, and lies sleeping in a ravine. Mowgli plans to kill the tiger.

Mowgli's plan was simple enough. All he wanted to do was to make a big circle uphill and get at the head of the ravine, and then take the bulls down it and catch Shere Khan between the bulls and the cows; for he knew that after a meal and a full drink Shere Khan would not be in any condition to fight or to clamber up the sides of the ravine. He was soothing the buffaloes now by voice, and Akela had dropped far to the rear, only whimpering once or twice to hurry the rear guard. It was a long, long circle, for they did not wish to get too near the ravine and give Shere Khan warning. At last Mowgli rounded up the bewildered herd at the head of the ravine on a grassy patch that sloped steeply down to the ravine itself. From that height you could see across the tops of the trees down to the plain below; but what Mowgli looked at was the sides of the ravine, and he saw with a great deal of satisfaction that they ran nearly straight up and down, while the vines and creepers that hung over them would give no foothold to a tiger who wanted to get out.

"Let them breathe, Akela," he said, holding up his hand. "They have not winded him yet. Let them breathe. I must tell Shere Khan who comes. We have him in the trap."

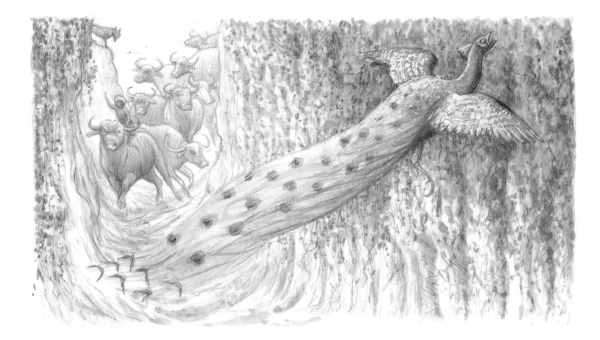

He put his hands to his mouth and shouted down the ravine—it was almost like shouting down a tunnel—and the echoes jumped from rock to rock.

After a long time there came back the drawling, sleepy snarl of a full-fed tiger just wakened.

"Who calls?" said Shere Khan, and a splendid peacock fluttered up out of the ravine screeching.

"I, Mowgli. Cattle thief, it is time to come to the Council Rock! Down—hurry them down, Akela! Down, Rama, down!"

The herd paused for an instant at the edge of the slope, but Akela gave tongue in the full hunting yell, and they pitched over one after the other, just as steamers shoot rapids, the sand and stones spurting up round them. Once started, there was no chance of stopping, and before they were fairly in the bed of the ravine Rama winded Shere Khan and bellowed.

"Ha! Ha!" said Mowgli, on his back. "Now thou knowest!'' and the torrent of black horns, foaming muzzles, and staring eyes whirled down the ravine like boulders in flood time: the weaker buffaloes being shouldered out to the sides of the ravine, where they tore through the creepers. They knew what the business was before them—the terrible charge of the buffalo herd, against which no tiger can hope to stand. Shere Khan heard the thunder of their hoofs, picked himself up, and lumbered down the ravine, looking from side to side for some way of escape; but the walls of the ravine were straight, and he had to keep on, heavy with his dinner and his drink, willing to do anything rather than fight. The herd splashed through the pool he had just left, bellowing till the narrow cut rang. Mowgli heard an answering bellow from the foot of the ravine, saw Shere Khan turn (the tiger knew

if the worst came to the worst it was better to meet the bulls than the cows with their calves), and then Rama tripped, stumbled, and went on again over something soft, and, with the bulls at his heels, crashed full into the other herd, while the weaker buffaloes were lifted clean off their feet by the shock of the meeting. That charge carried both herds out into the plain, goring and stamping and snorting. Mowgli watched his time, and slipped off Rama's neck, laying about him right and left with his stick.

"Quick, Akela! Break them up. Scatter them, or they will be fighting one another. Drive them away, Akela. *Hai*, Rama! *Hai! hai! hai!* my children. Softly now, softly! It is all over."

Akela and Gray Brother ran to and fro nipping the buffaloes' legs, and though the herd wheeled once to charge up the ravine again, Mowgli managed to turn Rama, and the others followed him to the wallows.

Shere Khan needed no more trampling. He was dead, and the kites were coming for him already

The Travelers and the Bear

by Aesop

A fat man and a thin man were walking together through a dark and gloomy forest.

"I'll be glad when we're out of here," said the thin man.

"Me too," said the fat man. "Who knows what wild beasts may be lurking. It's lucky there are two of us. We can stand by one another if danger threatens, can't we?"

"Oh, of course!" said the thin man. "I'd stand by you, my friend, to the bitter end. You can rely on that, I give you my solemn oath."

At that moment a large Bear came out of some bushes close by. Immediately the thin man, who was light and nimble, shinned up the nearest tree as quick as a monkey.

The fat man, slow and clumsy, did the only thing he could. He fell flat on his back on the forest floor and pretended to be dead. He lay absolutely still, eyes closed, and held his breath.

The Bear lumbered up and sniffed at the fat man, and then, supposing him indeed to be a corpse, lost interest and wandered away.

Once the Bear was out of sight, the thin man clambered down from his tree.

"What did the Bear say to you?" he asked his fat friend with a smile. "He was talking to you, I could see, for his mouth was close to your ear."

"He sent you a message," said the fat man drily. "He said to tell you that you're a rotten coward, and that in future I'd

67

better be careful about trusting a so-called friend, who gave his solemn oath, only to run away and leave me in the lurch."

MORAL: *Don't trust fine promises.*

The Tale of Mr. Jeremy Fisher

by Beatrix Potter

*Mr. Jeremy Fisher is a frog who lives in a little damp house
among the buttercups at the edge of a pond.*

The boat was round and green and very like the other lily leaves. It was tied to a water plant in the middle of the pond.

Mr. Jeremy took a reed pole, and pushed the boat out into open water.

"I know a good place for minnows," said Mr. Jeremy Fisher.

Mr. Jeremy stuck his pole into the mud and fastened his boat to it.

Then he settled himself cross-legged and arranged his fishing tackle. He had the dearest little red float. His rod was a tough stalk of grass, his line was a fine long white horse hair, and he tied a little wriggling worm at the end.

The rain trickled down his back, and for nearly an hour he stared at the float.

"This is getting tiresome, I think I should like some lunch," said Mr. Jeremy Fisher.

He punted back again amongst the water plants, and took some lunch out of his basket.

"I will eat a butterfly sandwich, and wait till the shower is over," said Mr. Jeremy Fisher.

A great big water beetle came up underneath the lily leaf and tweaked the toe of one of his galoshes.

Mr. Jeremy crossed his legs up shorter, out of reach, and went on eating his sandwich.

Once or twice something moved about with a rustle and a splash among the rushes at the side of the pond.

"I trust that is not a rat," said Mr. Jeremy; "I think I had better get away from here."

Mr. Jeremy shoved the boat out again a little way, and dropped in the bait. There was a bite almost directly; the float gave a tremendous bobbit!

"A minnow! A minnow! I have him by the nose!" cried Mr. Jeremy Fisher, jerking up his rod.

But what a horrible surprise! Instead of a smooth fat minnow, Mr. Jeremy landed little Jack Sharp the stickleback, covered with spines!

The stickleback floundered about the boat, pricking and snapping until he was quite out of breath. Then he jumped back into the water. And a shoal of other little fishes put their heads out, and laughed at Mr. Jeremy Fisher.

And while Mr. Jeremy sat disconsolately on the edge of his boat–sucking his sore fingers and peering down into the water–a *much* worse thing happened; a really *frightful* thing it would have been, if Mr. Jeremy had not been wearing a mackintosh!

A great big enormous trout came up–ker-pflop-p-p-p! with a splash–and it seized Mr. Jeremy with a snap, "Ow! Ow! Ow!"–and then turned and dived down to the bottom of the pond!

But the trout was so displeased with the taste of the mackintosh, that in less than half a minute it spat him out again; and the only thing it swallowed was Mr. Jeremy's galoshes.

Black Beauty

by Anna Sewell

Black Beauty was published in 1877. It is the story of the life of a horse, a story seen through the horse's eyes. They look on the two sides of human nature—the kindness and the cruelty.
Black Beauty himself has come down in the world, suffering greatly the while, but now, at the last, he is once again in good hands. Joe Green, who as a lad once, through ignorance, nearly caused the horse's death, here, after many years, comes face to face with Black Beauty once more.

In the morning a smart-looking young man came for me. At first he looked pleased, but when he saw my knees, he said in a disappointed voice: "I didn't think, sir, you would have recommended my ladies a blemished horse like this."

"Handsome is that handsome does," said my master. "You are only taking him on trial, and I am sure you will do fairly by him, young man; and if he is not as safe as any horse you ever drove, send him back."

I was led home, placed in a comfortable stable, fed, and left to myself.

The next day, when my groom was cleaning my face, he said: "That is just like the star that Black Beauty had, and he is much the same height too; I wonder where he is now."

A little farther on he came to the place in my neck where I was bled, and where a little knot was left in the skin. He almost started, and began to look me over carefully, talking to himself.

"White star in the forehead, one white foot on the off side, this little knot just in that place;" then, looking at the middle of my back—"and as I am alive, there is that little patch of white hair that John used to call 'Beauty's threepenny-bit.' It *must* be Black Beauty! Why, Beauty! Beauty! do you know me, little Joe Green that almost killed you?" And he began patting and patting me as if he was quite overjoyed.

I could not say that I remembered him, for now he was a fine grown young fellow with black whiskers and a man's voice, but I was sure that he knew me, and that he was Joe Green; so I was very glad. I put my nose up to him, and tried to say that we were friends. I never saw a man so pleased.

The Sheep-Pig

by Dick King-Smith

At the beginning of the story of the Sheep-Pig, Farmer Hogget
wins a little pig at the village fair. Here the piglet is introduced to Fly,
the collie, and her pups.

"Hello," she said. "Who are you?"

"I'm a Large White," said the piglet.

"Blimey!" said one of the puppies. "If that's a large white, what's a small one like?" And they all four sniggered.

"Be quiet!" snapped Fly. "Just remember that five minutes ago you didn't even know what a pig was." And to the piglet she said kindly, "I expect that's your breed, dear. I meant, what's your name?"

"I don't know," said the piglet.

"Well, what did your mother call you, to tell you apart from your brothers and sisters?" said Fly and then wished she hadn't, for at the mention of his family the piglet began to look distinctly unhappy. His little forehead wrinkled and he gulped and his voice trembled as he answered.

"She called us all the same."

"And what was that, dear?"

"Babe," said the piglet, and the puppies began to giggle until their mother silenced them with a growl.

"But that's a lovely name," she said. "Would you like us to call you that? It'll make you feel more at home."

At this last word the little pig's face fell even further.

"I want my mom," he said very quietly.

At that instant the collie made up her mind that she would foster this unhappy child.

"Go out into the yard and play," she said to the puppies, and she climbed to the top of the straw stack and jumped over the rail and down into the loose-box beside the piglet.

"Listen, Babe," she said. "You've got to be a brave boy. Everyone has to leave their mother, it's all part of growing up. I did so, when I was your age, and my puppies will have to leave me quite soon. But I'll look after you. If you like." Then she licked his little snout with a warm tongue, her plumed tail wagging.

"There. Is that nice?" she said.

The Donkey, the Ape and the Mole

by Aesop

A Donkey was worried because he had no horns. He looked about the fields and saw cows and goats with fine horns, and he wandered into the forest and saw deer with even finer ones.

In the forest the Donkey met an Ape. The Ape was worried because he had no tail.

He looked around and saw foxes and squirrels with beautiful bushy tails, and even the Donkey, he noticed, had a tail, even if it was a rather funny one like a bellpull.

"It's a rotten life," he said in a melancholy voice.

"It is indeed," said the Donkey grumpily. "It's not as if I'm asking for much. Just a decent pair of horns, that's all. You can't blame me for feeling wretched."

"You can't blame me for feeling miserable either," grumbled the Ape. "All I want is a nice long tail. It's not as if I'm asking for much."

They looked sadly at one another.

Just then the earth in front of them heaved up into a little hill and out of the top of it came a black snout.

The Donkey and the Ape watched as a Mole emerged and moved clumsily toward them, bumping into first one and then the other.

"Watch out!" brayed the Donkey, and "Look where you're going!" chattered the Ape.

"Sorry," said the Mole cheerfully. "Specially as you two chaps sound so unhappy over what you lack. Me, I'm just blind."

MORAL: *Don't complain—others are worse off than you.*

The Sheep-Pig

by Dick King-Smith

PART II

Two dogs have been worrying the sheep, but the Sheep-Pig drives them away. In the middle of the field lies a ewe that the dogs have brought down.

The field was clear, and Babe suddenly came back to his senses. He turned and hurried to the fallen ewe, round whom, now that the dogs had gone, the horrified flock was beginning to gather in a rough circle. She lay still now, as Babe stood panting by her side, a draggled side where the worriers had pulled at it, and suddenly he realized. It was Ma!

"Ma?" he cried. "Ma! Are you all right?"

She did not seem too badly hurt. He could not see any gaping wounds, though blood was coming from one ear where the dogs had bitten it.

The old ewe opened an eye. Her voice, when she spoke, was as hoarse as ever, but now not much more than a whisper.

"Hello, young un," she said.

Babe dropped his head and gently licked the ear to try to stop the bleeding, and some blood stuck to his snout.

"Can you get up?" he asked.

For some time Ma did not answer, and he looked anxiously at her, but the eye that he could see was still open.

"I don't reckon," she said.

"It's all right, Ma," Babe said. "The wolves have gone, far away."

"Far, far, fa-a-a-a-a-ar!" chorused the flock.

"And Fly and the boss will soon be here to look after you."

Ma made no answer or movement. Only her ribs jumped to the thump of her tired old heart.

"You'll be all right, honestly you will," said Babe.

"Oh ar," said Ma, and then the eye closed and the ribs jumped no more.

"Oh Ma!" said Babe, and "Ma! Ma! Ma-a-a-a-a-a!" mourned the flock, as the Land Rover came up the lane.

Farmer Hogget had heard nothing of the worrying—the field was too far away, the wind in the wrong direction—but he had been anxious, and so by now had Fly, because Pig was nowhere to be found.

The moment they entered the field both man and dog could see that something was terribly wrong. Why else was the flock so obviously distressed, panting and gasping and dishevelled? Why had they formed that ragged circle, and what was in the middle of it? Farmer Hogget strode forward, Fly before him parting the ring to make way, only to see a sight that struck horror into the hearts of both.

There before them lay a dead ewe, and bending over it was the pig, his snout almost touching the outstretched neck, a snout, they saw, that was stained with blood.

White Fang

by Jack London

White Fang is half-wolf, and here, in the terrible story of a fight,
he is matched (by cruel men) against the bulldog, Cherokee.

As the impetus that carried Cherokee forward died down, he continued to go forward of his own volition, in a swift, bowlegged run. Then White Fang struck. A cry of startled admiration went up. He had covered the distance and gone in more like a cat than a dog; and with the same catlike swiftness he had slashed with his fangs and leaped clear.

The bulldog was bleeding back of one ear from a rip in his thick neck. He gave no sign, did not even snarl, but turned and followed after White Fang. The display on both sides, the quickness of the one and the steadiness of the other, had excited the partisan spirit of the crowd, and the men were making new bets and increasing original bets. Again, and yet again, White Fang sprang in, slashed, and got away untouched; and still his strange foe followed after him, without too great haste, not slowly, but deliberately and determinedly, in a businesslike sort of way. There was purpose in his method—something for him to do that he was intent upon doing and from which nothing could distract him.

His whole demeanor, every action, was stamped with this purpose. It puzzled White Fang. Never had he seen such a dog. It had no hair protection. It was soft, and bled easily. There was no thick mat of fur to baffle White Fang's teeth as they were often baffled by dogs of his own breed. Each time that his teeth struck they sank easily into the yielding flesh, while the animal did not seem able to defend itself. Another disconcerting thing was that it made no outcry, such as he had been accustomed to with the other dogs he had fought. Beyond a growl or a grunt, the dog took its punishment silently. And never did it flag in its pursuit of him.

Not that Cherokee was slow. He could turn and whirl swiftly enough, but White Fang was never there. Cherokee was puzzled, too. He had never fought before with a dog with which he could not close. The desire to close had always been mutual. But here was a dog that kept at a distance, dancing and dodging here and there and all about. And when it did get its teeth into him, it did not hold on but let go instantly and darted away again.

But White Fang could not get at the soft underside of the throat. The bulldog stood too short, while its massive jaws were an added protection. White Fang darted in and out unscathed, while Cherokee's wounds increased. Both sides of his neck and head were ripped and slashed. He bled freely, but showed no signs of being disconcerted. He continued his plodding pursuit, though once, for the moment baffled, he came to a full stop and blinked at the men who looked on, at the same time wagging his stump of a tail as an expression of his willingness to fight.

In that moment White Fang was in upon him and out, in passing ripping his trimmed remnant of an ear. With a slight manifestation of anger, Cherokee took up the pursuit again, running on the inside of the circle White Fang was making, and striving to fasten his deadly grip on White Fang's throat. The bulldog missed by a hair's breadth, and cries of praise went up as White Fang doubled suddenly out of danger in the opposite direction.

The time went by. White Fang still danced on, dodging and doubling, leaping in and out, and ever inflicting damage. And still the bulldog, with grim certitude, toiled after him. Sooner or later he would accomplish his purpose, get the grip that would win the battle. In the meantime he accepted all the punishment the other could deal him. His tufts of ears had become tassels, his neck and shoulders were slashed in a score of places, and his very lips were cut and bleeding—all from those lightning snaps that were beyond his foreseeing and guarding.

Time and again White Fang had attempted to knock Cherokee off his feet, but the difference in their height was too great. Cherokee was too squat, too close to the ground. White Fang tried the trick once too often. The chance came in one of his quick doublings and counter-circlings. He caught Cherokee with head turned away as he whirled more slowly. His shoulder was exposed. White Fang drove in upon it, but his own shoulder was high above, while he struck with such force that his momentum carried him on across over the other's body. For the first time in his fighting history, men saw White Fang lose his footing. His body turned a half-somersault in the air, and he would have landed on his back had he not twisted, catlike, still in the air, in the effort to bring his feet to the earth. As it was, he struck heavily on his side. The next instant he was on his feet, but in that instant Cherokee's teeth closed on his throat.

The bulldog never lets go his grip, but White Fang survives thanks to the interference of a kindly man, survives indeed to live long and happily at the last.

Noah's Brother

by Dick King-Smith

PART II

The dove Peace has returned to the Ark. This time she carries something in her beak. Noah calls the family to look.

"Behold!" he cried to the family.

And they beheld.

"It's a dove," said Ham, who wasn't very bright.

Japheth and Shem were not much better.

"It's got something in its beak," said one.

"Looks like a twig with leaves on it," said the other.

Mrs. Noah was the best of a bad bunch. She was after all a cook, and cooks used oil, and oil came from olives.

"It's an olive twig," she said.

"Of course it's an olive twig!" roared Noah. "Any fool can see that. But where did it come from?"

"Off an olive tree?" said Ham hopefully.

"Well, what does that mean, you dolt?" shouted Noah. "Can none of you see what it means?"

His brick-red face turned purple.

"Begone!" he bellowed at the family.

And they bewent.

Only Yessah stood his ground, though he was shaking with fear at his brother's anger.

"Well?" shouted Noah.

"It m-means that the Flood is beginning to go down. Somewhere, there is a tree sticking up above the water."

"You're not as stupid as you look," said Noah.

"P-please," said Yessah, "can I have my dove back?"

"Take your bird," growled Noah, "but I shall want it again, one week from today."

There was great excitement as news of the olive twig spread round the boat, the boat in which they had all been confined for so long, cramped, damp, and often seasick. All the animals were indeed heartily sick of the sea and longing to stretch their legs, or their wings, or their coils once again.

"How we will run!" cried the gazelles.

"How we will soar!" cried the eagles.

"How we will hop!" cried the kangaroos.

"How we will climb!" cried the monkeys.

"How we will eat ants!" cried the anteaters.

The ants just cried.

Remember

"So-and-so wouldn't hurt a fly."
How often have we heard somebody say
These words. But is it true, say I?
Not many of us live a single day
And don't condemn some living thing to die.

Spiders and silverfish and fleas,
The wasp, the slug, the woodlouse and the snail
In homes and gardens take their ease,
But many will not live to tell the tale.
We are not kind to creatures such as these.

What in the world are we to do?
We kill, if not on purpose, by mistake.
Not hurt a fly? That can't be true,
But let us try, for everybody's sake,
To be more kindly. I shall try. Will you?

Dick King-Smith

KILLOFF

SLUG PE

Reading List

If you have enjoyed the excerpts from stories I selected for THE ANIMAL PARADE, you may like to read the complete book. And in case you would like to read more animal stories, I have made a list of some other books I have enjoyed. I suggest that you go along to your local bookshop or, if copies are not available, to your local library and ask the assistant to help you find copies of the ones that interest you. Some were written a long time ago and others are more recent, some are easy to read, some are more difficult, but they all have one thing in common – their authors love and understand animals and convey this in their stories.

Richard Adams
Watership Down

Aesop
Aesop's Fables

Hilaire Belloc
The Bad Child's Book of Beasts

Lewis Carroll
Alice's Adventures in Wonderland

Gerald Durrell
The Bafut Beagles

T.S. Eliot
*Old Possum's Book of
Practical Cats*

Jack Goodman, editor
*The Fireside Book of
Dog Stories*

Kenneth Grahame
The Wind in the Willows

Selina Hastings, reteller
Reynard the Fox

Richard Jefferies
The Amateur Poacher
The Gamekeeper at Home

Dick King-Smith
Babe: The Gallant Pig
Harry's Mad
Noah's Brother
Pigs Might Fly

Rudyard Kipling
The Jungle Book
Just So Stories

Jack London
White Fang

Walter de la Mare
Collected Poems

A.A. Milne
Winnie-the-Pooh
The House at Pooh Corner

Alan Moorehead
No Room in the Ark

Beatrix Potter
Tales

Ernest Thompson Seton
Lives of the Hunted
Wild Animals I Have Known

Anna Sewell
Black Beauty

G.B. Stern
The Ugly Dachshund

E.B. White
Charlotte's Web

Gilbert White
*The Natural History
of Selborne*

J.H. Williams
Elephant Bill

Henry Williamson
Salar the Salmon
Tarka the Otter

Acknowledgements

We would like to thank the following for permission to include
excerpts from their books:

Viking Penguin Inc. for *Daggie Dogfoot* by Dick King-Smith

HarperCollins Publishers for *Elephant Bill* by James Howard Williams

The Society of Authors, London, for *Five Eyes* by Walter de la Mare

Random House Inc. for *Harry's Mad* and *The Sheep-Pig* by Dick King-Smith

Frederick Warne & Co. for *The Tale of Jeremy Fisher* by Beatrix Potter

The Estate of the late Henry Williamson and The Bodley Head for *Tarka the Otter*

Every effort has been made to trace copyright holders but if any omissions have been made,
please let us know so that we may put this right in the next edition.

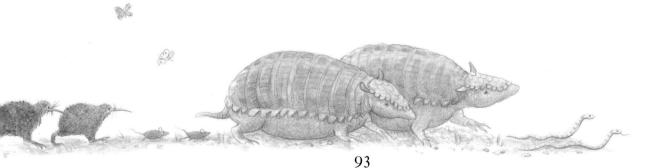